TITLE

# THE ALPHA'S CHANCE

# Chapter 1

My paws hit the mudlike soil. The natural air blowing in my face and going through my dull chestnut hide. As I check out my environmental factors I see the enormous emerald pine trees. I see birds taking off in the sky. Gracious yet the sky, it is delightful. Its blended in with various shades of blue, pink, and yellow appearance that it is sunrise. I halt abruptly briefly, shut my eyes and spotlight on what I can hear. I hear the streaming brook that is about a pretty far. I can hear a couple of hatchlings requiring their mom. A gathering of squirrels pursuing another. In this time, I'm loaded up with tranquil euphoria. Yet, that is completely destroyed when I hear him coming towards me. He draws nearer constantly and I set myself up in an unpretentious guarded position prepared for his assault. I hear him seize me, however before he can get his hands on me, I have him on his back lying exposed.

Fuck! Come on sister, truly? Caleb, my more established sibling asks me through the midlink.

Ya know, I dont know why you continue to attempt to surprise me. It won't ever work. I connect him back with a laugh.

Ugh! You're no reasonable. He answers and I can detect him feigning exacerbation at me.

Caleb, quit acting infantile. What do you need? I ask, with a trace of irritation in my voice.

Oof sister. Father just advised me to advise you that preparation begins soon and to go to his office after you get tidied up. He says while escaping my hold and shaking his hide out.

Alright. Well give me a couple of moments and I'll see you at the preparation fields. I answer, and after that he gestures and runs back from where he came from.

I remain there for a couple of moments just to think, and before I go let me inroduce myself. I go by Alice Clara

Blackwood, I am the girl of Alpha Emmett and Luna Isobel Blackwood, the heads of the most remarkable pack on the planet, the Cresent Moon pack, after the Royal Pack obviously. Furthermore tragically the more youthful sister by five years of Caleb Natheniel Blackwood, the following Alpha. I love him, I truly do, yet once in a while he can be an undeniable irritation. At any rate... I'm 21 years of age with a Bachealors degree in Business. You might ask how, well lets simply say that I avoided all of highschool and went directly to school. One thing I don't actually like with regards to myself is my stature, I'm five foot three for Christs purpose! Altough it proves to be useful when me and different champions of our pack fight during preparing. It expands my versatility and speed. I love music, preparing, cooking and baking, perusing, and I think there's nothing else to it.

Are you certain you're not missing something. A voice rings in my mind

Gracious yes! My wolf Anya, how is it that I could disregard her.

You better fucking love me bitch. She shouts.

Obviously I love you Anya, quit being so ill humored. I react and can feel her leave towards the rear of my psyche.

Proceeding... I play the piano and the cello, my mother encouraged me how to play the piano when I was the age of five. Then, at that point, after four years I began to encourage myself how to play the cello with a lot of books and youtube recordings. With respect to preparing, Ha! I might be little, yet don't underrate me. I put forth a truly valiant effort. I was prepared by the most elite. Ezekiel was the head fighter from the Royal Pack until he was shipped off us for a new beginning. Ezekiel lost his mate from a rebel assault. She was close to the boundary bringing the champions some lunch utilizing a neglected alternate way, however a rebel assaulted her and killed her before she got inside a consultation distance. I don't have the foggiest idea how he is taking care of it so indeed, I would never envision losing my mate and live with the prospect that I would never save them. Observing my mate would be a little glimpse of heaven, for werewolves, you can find your mate once you turn 16. Most will observe their mate immediately, yet not me. For hell's sake, even Caleb observed his mate Fiona at 19 and they are anticipating a fourth little guy in 90 days.

Since the time I was ten years of age Ezekiel has shown me all that he knows. From a wide range of hand to hand battle to firing weapons, toxophilism, and tossing blades. The more I advanced the harder preparing got. At the point when I was 15 he began blindfolding me so I could stregnthen my human faculties and I could be similarly just about as ready as Anya. There wasn't a lot preparing for when I was in my wolf structure, Anya was at that point solid and covert. I basically pin it on the Alpha blood going through my veins.

Since the time I gratuated from school I've been assisting my mom with her Luna obligations. So for the beyond three years in the wake of preparing I go visit the pack's emergency clinic, nursing home, and keep an eye on the numerous organizations our pack individuals own with her. Despite the fact that I'm not exceeding everyone's expectations next Alpha my folks actually imagined that I ought to get a similar preparing as Caleb and I was glad to do as such.

I get up from the beginning, out my hide and begin running home to prepare. At the point when I return home and saw that everybody has gone to work, I surge up the steps and into my space to take out my garments from my wardrobe. I wind up picking a couple of charcoal shaded high waisted tights, a light dark consistent games bra, and a white tie up tank top for certain dark running shoes. I put everything on and tie my hair into a tight high pig tail. When I completed that, I head out through the secondary passage and towards the preparation fields.

Chapter 02

Following a few minutes of strolling, I show up at the preparation fields. It is a ten section of land real estate parcel were the heroes train and fight in both wolf and human structure. There is additionally a 43,700 squarefoot substantial structure where there is likewise space to fight. It likewise incorporates a wide range of exercise center hardware and a shooting range.

"Alice!" A male voice that I perceive as Ezekiels, calls me. "You're late."

As I check my watch I say, "No I'm not. I'm exactly on schedule."

"Alice" he states evidently. "You know how it is. Being early is being on schedule and being o-"

"On time is in effect late. No doubt better believe it, I know." I interupt and end with an irritated moan.

"Great. Then, at that point, we should not burn through any longer time and get everything rolling. I heard you had a gathering with the Alpha subsequent to preparing." Ezekiel commented.

I gestured and we returned to work. At the point when Ezekiel moved here he prepared our most grounded heroes so they could later show the others. When they were prepared he would regulate and still train a few heroes until he began to by and by prepare Caleb and I. Eversince Caleb turned 18 he began to prepare with the heroes as a result of his future as Alpha. Ezekiel has shown me such a lot of I can beat Caleb, Gamma Alex, Beta Noah, and Ezekiel himself. Albeit out of the multiple occasions we have fought, I've just beat him multiple times, which is very little. A portion of the fighters would joke that I should fight with father, yet I've never had the guts to inquire.

After five laps around the field, fifteen sparrings, versatility excercises, bows and arrows and shooting training, I say my farewell to certain champions and Ezekiel and advance home. At the point when I return home, I shower and get dressed. I chose to wear some light blue thin pants, a white sweater, and a hazelnut raincoat for the cold fall climate with matching high heel bootie boots. Then, at that point, I put my hair up in a tight low bun with two strands of hair outlining my face. With respect to cosmetics I simply utilize some mascara and apply a touch of lip gleam. Mother consistently let me know that I shouldn't utilize an excessive amount of cosmetics and to show my actual magnificence.

When I'm prepared, I head down to the kitchen and get one of those Naked organic product juices and a ham and cheddar sandwhich that my mother makes me regular. I know its not much for a werewolf, but rather assuming it were dependent upon me I would simply drink my juice or eat nothing by any means. In the wake of eating, I clean my teeth and head to the packhouse.

The house is huge . It has eight rooms each with its own restroom, four on the subsequent floor and the other four on the third floor. The vast majority of the pack live in their own homes and we had assembled a high rise for the unmated wolves. The pack has in excess of 400 individuals. The main individuals who stay in the packhouse are guests from different packs, however everybody visits occasionally to hang out. It has a famlily room, lounge area that seats 16 individuals, a monstrous kitchen that the culinary specialists possess, a game room, theater room, and the workplaces of the Alpha, Beta, and Gamma that are on the fourth floor. I go up the three stairwells and thump on the oak swinging doors that were toward the finish of the corridor driving into the Alphas office.

"Come in." My fathers voice requested.

At the point when I opened one of the entryways I saw that my mother and Caleb were at that point there, validating the previous premonitions I had when I was on the last advance of the steps. When I was totally inside the workplace I shut the entryway, then, at that point, offered them every one of the a delicate grin and a "hello".

"Great morning darling, how was preparing?" mother asked happily. My mom was consistently an excellent lady. She has brown reddish-brown hair down to her shoulders and dark green eyes that help you to remember the backwoods. She is minuscule in stature, yet at the same time an inch or two taller than me. My father then again is a lot taller than us going up to six foot one like Caleb. In actuality, Caleb resembles a duplicate of father, both have dull earthy colored hair like mine however not simultaneously and hazel eyes.

"It was incredible! Much obliged for asking." I answer cheerfully.

"Alright father, we are for the most part here, what did you want to tell us?" Caleb asked brutally and irritated. I can perceive he misses Fiona and his little guys, they are on the whole inseperable, its difficult to get them separated. Particularly Caleb because of the way that Fiona is pregnant once more.

"Gracious yes! Indeed, I simply needed to tell both of you that Alpha Tremblay from the Blood Moon Pack will be coming and remaining for the end of the week alongside his Beta. He called requesting to meet and requested assistance with a rebel issue, simply some direction. He was likewise expecting to have the option to set a coalition between the packs. They show up in a couple of hours and afterward we will allow them to get comfortable before the gathering that is booked for five. You can do your typical schedules, however ensure you are here by then, at that point. Additionally Alice, could you set up certain rewards for the gathering, please? Nothing too substantial on the grounds that we eat after. Talking about supper, could you likewise advise the cooks to set up a dinner for eight individuals? Noah and Alex will join aswell." My dad generously inquired.

"Obviously, not an issue." I acknowledged with a gesture.

"Pause," Caleb began. "Alpha Tremblay-as in Alpha Jackson Tremblay? Isn't his pack close to the Royal Pack?"

"Indeed and Yes." Dad affirmed.

Mother chose to toll in and says, "I heard that he is probably the most youthful alpha in this side of the half of the globe. He is 23 and took over at eighteen. It's likewise said that he makes a significant astounding pioneer." Dad snarls at that and mother chuckles then, at that point, murmurs something in his ear, however I dont imagine that I need to know what she is saying. The entire time we discussed this Alpha, I could feel Anya mixing in my mind yet I disregarded the inclination.

Caleb jeers and fights, "Well I heard that he is an incredible man prostitute."

"CALEB NATHANIEL BLACKWOOD! Watch that mouth of yours!" Mom admonished. I make a decent attempt to conceal my giggle, watchword attempt, following a couple of moments I burst out dismissing my butt. Mother never hollered, yet assuming you accomplish something she would rather avoid then amazing good fortune. It's great that Caleb is her child or, more than likely she would have accomplished something wosre. Despite the fact that it was a basic affront mother, in the same way as other different moms, instructed us to not make a judgment too quickly and to treat others the manner in which you need to be dealt with. Which I totally concur with, individuals shouldn't simply accept things, they ought to get to realize the individual prior to causing something that could damage an expected relationship, whatever it very well might be.

I chilled off and mother and I left to do our every day adjusts. Caleb remained to go over some Alpha stuff, father anticipates venturing down in a couple of months. When we were done, it was 4:30 and I returned home to set up the rewards. I additionally needed to advise the gourmet specialists to plan supper.

Hello Sofie! Could you set up a supper for eight please. Something straightforward however filling. I connected Sofie the head culinary specialist. She was an astonishing cook, at whatever point I was at the packhouse as a little guy I would watch her cook. At the point when she thought I was full grown enough she began giving me cooking and baking illustrations.

Obviously dear, what about steak with cooked veggies and for dessert I can make your top choice. Sofie advertised. This lady realizes me better than I do with regards to food. One day she caused me the most heavenly strawberry cheesecake I to have at any point tasted. I realize its very basic, yet the taste was incredible.

Sounds stunning, says thanks to Sophie! After a little discussion I had all that I wanted out to make the rewards. I made a natural product plate, vegetable plate, and a cheddar plate. I was so focused on making the plate I didn't know about what time it was. When I completed it was 4:58. I immediately put the plate in a major cardboard sack alongside water and plastic cups and ran towards the packhouse. It planned to take me somewhat longer since I was in heels fortunately they were thick so I wouldn't be past the point of no return.

'Goodness my goddess. Father will kill me!' I thought. He seldom welcomes me to his gatherings with different Alphas. Since I consider it, he never has, and presently I demolished the odds of getting welcomed to another.

I show up at the packhouse and race up the steps to the workplace. Anya was drawing more fretful the nearer we were, however I was so engrossed about not being any longer late that I wasn't focusing on whatever else. I hammer the entryways open, "So sorry I'm late, the rewards " I was then hit with the most inebriating aroma on the planet, citrius and sandalwood, it was so great it made me inside groan. Then, at that point, all of the abrupt the man that the fragrance has a place with is before me and humble snarls out, "MINE!"

Chapter 03

JACKSON POV

I'm getting out of the shower when I hear development in my room. I stroll into my room in my towel and observe Courtney, one of the young ladies known for dozing around with individuals from the pack. She loves to burn through my time and rub herself on me and my bed while wearing a scanty pair of red lingere. At whatever point sees me, she generally attempts to allure me into laying down with her. And keeping in mind that most young ladies in the end become familiar with their place and let me be, she never appears to need to release me. As though that were sufficiently not, she additionally prefers to imagine we are mates and that she will be Luna since I made out with her one time four years prior. I continue telling her that it made next to no difference to me since we were youthful and it was uniquely to remove my psyche from my new alpha obligations, however she never needs to release it. In the event that she weren't really impolite to the wide range of various shewolves, and would quit discoloring her standing by dozing around so much, I may like her only a tad. Possibly then, at that point, could I think of her as deserving of the luna position. Notwithstanding this, Courtney is my top female fighter and I realize that she can ensure this pack if she somehow happened to be luna. With the steady rebel assaults we have been having, I can't have a mate who can't ensure themselves. However with every one of my obligations, observing a mate isn't among the highest point of my prority list, yet I do long to have that association that having a mate gives.

"Hello child, I was figuring we could have a good time earlier today. I trust you like what you see." She swaggers towards me, measuring my buldge. I snatch her wrist fuming, totally offended that she would take action on me like that knowing as Alpha I might have her tossed in the cells in an occasion.

Typically pack disciplines resemble local area administration and I seldom at any point need to 'rebuff' a pack part. "What do you believe that is no joke?" I gripped my jaw in disappointment. Scarcely allowing me to complete my sentence, she has the dauntlessness to smile and fire fondling my arm, my body developing hot out of frustration, and perhaps only a bit of piece of excitement. "Just idea we would have some good times before you needed to leave, and don't say you didn't missed me child." She answered honestly, he face shaping into a sulk. This is making me need to rip her arm off significantly more as my wolf and I are now flinching at the way that anybody, yet our mate would dare contact us in a suductive way. My wolf, Jax, tolls in that, If there is anything she rises it assuredly isn't my dick, rather my pulse from simply checking out her.

"I figure its to your greatest advantage to leave now and leave," yet similarly as I say that she broadens her eyes in entertainment and I would already be able to tell she is considering something. Similarly as I expected shes taken her free arm off me and moved it to the rear of her bra endeavoring to unclasp the snare. In the nick of time my beta, Derek, strolls in as I as of now mindlinked him when I saw Courtney. I gesture in appreciation to him as he removes her from my room while shes concocting a wide range of reasons with respect to why she shouldn't leave, however my beta and I both realize whatever emerges from her mouth does not merit paying attention to. I shake my head and advance toward my storage room where I get clothing for the gathering I have sometime in the afternoon with Alpha Emmett Blackwood from the Cresent Moon Pack.

I get done with preparing in a dull blue button up shirt and dark dress jeans. I go down the stairs to the kitchen and I see Derek sitting on one of the bar stools behind the island. Strolling towards the refrigerator to get a jug of water he makes a sound as if to speak and begins, "She never stops, isn't that right? What's more you'll never get it over with and screw her, will you?" I glare at his inquiries and answer, "Derek, you know how I feel about mating with different females. It's not reasonable that most guys have effectively mated with others and their mates have consistently been sitting tight for their mate." Listening to my reaction he feigns exacerbation, however gestures in comprehension. To change the point I order, "What is todays morning report?"

"Well preparing worked out positively, the beginners don't suck and are quick students. I figure we will have more prepared champions quicker than expecting. I checked in with the watches and they say that nothing has been strange and no rebels have been seen. I trust everything is stuffed and all set because Grayson be here shortly." Derek reports certainly. Grayson is my gamma and my dearest companion separated from Derek. I entrust these men with my life and they entrust me with theirs. "Okay, thanks man."

Not excessively long later, we hear a blare before the house and immeadiately realize that it is Grayson. I don't reside in the packhouse, I like my own security, so I fabricated a house not that ages ago. However, as seen recently, I don't get quite a bit of it. It has five rooms each with its own washroom, kitchen, dinning room, and a lounge. As we stroll down the steps, Grayson was escaping the vehicle and running towards us. Assisting us with placing our things in the storage compartment he states, "Well folks, the vehicle is has a full tank of gas and there are tidbits and water in the rearward sitting arrangements. I set up the GPS and you ought to be arrivng in around three hours. The tank should last you the entire excursion however I would recommend topping off it when there is a quater left for good measure. It should likewise not surge you to observing a service station returning." Grayson was consistently similar to an organizer, he prepares and figures out how to prepare everything. He has assisted with such countless things like gathering with the pack, pack runs, pack festivities. Normally the Luna would be the one to arrange these things and have different sorts of obligations, however until further notice Grayson lands that position and he dominates at it. At the point when we have everything in and hammer the storage compartment shut, I remind Grayson, "Recollect. Assuming anything is wild call me, regardless of whether it be by means of mindlink or telephone. Additionally, the Morris family is moving into the new house close the packhouse. I let them know I would sen-" I get intturupted by Grayson when he says, "I know Jackson, I was the person who aided arrangement their moving. Presently go, or, more than likely you'll be late and won't establish a decent connection with Alpha Blackwood. I heard he was a terrifying man and I don't need him to despise us. In addition in addition to the fact that you must intrigue him his child as well, who I question that he doesn't have a say in case we get an opportunity at coalition."

"OK. OK, we're going. Much obliged Gray. We will see you in two or three days." I say in a quieted tone. I realize he can deal with the pack in my nonappearance, however that doesn't prevent me from agonizing over my pack. I see Grays' eyes load up with entertainment and I prepare myself for the words that emerge from his mouth, "All things considered, bring us back a luna will ya?" I inside snarl at his remark, yet keep an unemotional appearance all over. Its been right around ten years I actually haven't tracked down my mate. My storage room is half unfilled and there is a vacant vanity in my restroom, both holding on to be utilized for the one the Moon Goddess has favored me with.

Dereks voice breaks my line of reasoning when he says, "He's right, we will be late. We should take off now." I gesture my head in understanding and we go into the vehicle, lock in, and head towards the Crescent Moon Pack.

*Three Hours Later*

We show up at the Cresent Moon Pack and are leaded to their packhouse. It is very more modest than our own, yet they have such countless houses and lofts that it would check out to not need to stress over having a large enough house. I escape the vehicle and I can feel a solid air that I know has a place with the Alpha. I go to see Alpha Emmett remaining before the house with a more youthful man that looks a couple of years more seasoned than me. I expect he is the future Alpha Caleb. I approach them and present myself, "Hi, I go by Jackson. I'm the Alpha of the Blood Moon Pack and this is my Beta, Derek." I report pointing towards Derek who gives the smallest bow. The Alpha grins and shakes my hand as he says, "Its good to meet you Alpha Jackson and Beta Derek. Welcome to the Crescent Moon Pack, I trust you didn't have any difficulty in transit here. This is my child and future alpha Caleb. You will meet my mate and girl some other time when the gathering starts." Daughter? When did he have a girl. Derek joins me and says in a confounded tone, I have never heard that he had a girl. Neither have different Alphas. Do you think he is concealing her? His inquiry interests me and I right away need to find out about her. Emmett proceeds, "Indeed, let me show you to your rooms."

He shows us to our rooms and lets us settly in before the gathering begins, Jax begins pacing my brain and I can't make him stop. Will you stop as of now, you are giving me a migraine. Move past with whatever is at the forefront of your thoughts, I can't bear to be diverted during this gathering. I snapped, however he disregarded me and continued to pace in my psyche. I snort irritated at my wolf and go to the washroom and splah my face with cold water to loosen up a bit.

After seemingly hours, it was the ideal opportunity for the gathering. Derek thumps on my entryway and we head up to the Alphas office that is higher up. I thump on the entryway and recieve a 'Come in'. I stroll in and see Alpha Emmett, Caleb, and a lady remaining adjacent to him, and two different men. "Alpha Jackson, this is my mate and wonderful luna Isobel, my Beta Noah, and my Gamma Alex." he says with such profound love in his eyes discussing his mate and trust towards his right and left in order. Luna Isobel daintily becomes flushed, however doesn't stop for a second to offer her hand which I take and shake as she remarks, "It is extraordinary to at last meet you!"

"Similarly Luna Isobel, this is my Beta Derek," she offers him a little grin and we as a whole head to the huge meeting table along the edge of his office.

I notice the Alpha Blackwood check out the clock that is holding tight the divider that read 5:01 and stress was spreading across his face. I check out the room and see what he is stressed over, little girl hasn't showed up. An additional couple of moments passed and I was simply beginning to get irritated. I was going to shout out until I was hit with the solid lovely fragrance of energy leafy foods. It was the most flavorful smell I have at any point smelled and I never needed to quit smelling it, it resembled paradise. The fragrance was getting progressively strong until the entryway pummeled open astounding we all and afterward the most heavenly voice I have at any point heard apologized saying, "So sorry I'm late, the rewards " in the time she was speaking I got up and went dtraight to the holy messenger that was remaining at the entryway and snarled, "MINE!"

This heavenly messenger was lovely, long chestnut earthy colored hair, the most profound blue eyes that I could never get worn out seeing, light complexion, little stout lips that I need to tastes so gravely, in case she would let me. I peer down at her chest and can see her round bosoms that are the ideal size to cup in my grasp and stunning little butt that will torment me for the remainder of my life. I take her all in start to finish and I can see her wriggle under my look, which turns me on. I notice that she is tiny and needs to incline her head back to investigate my eyes. She has the tallness of a kid! Peering down at her I feel the unexpected desire to shield her from any mischief, regardless of whether it's simply a little subterranean insect creeping on the ground. For what reason would the Moon Goddess favor me with a mate right now? I incline down and put my face on the evildoer of her neck to remember her aroma and I feel her shiver, which make me grin. I'm happy that I have such an impact on me. The following couple of moments that we take in eachothers fragrances, we overlooked the remainder of the world unitl somebody makes a sound as if to speak and someone else screeches.

"Gracious my Goddess! My dear, congrats!" Luna Isobel screeches with fervor. She somewhat helps me to remember my own mom. I peer down at my lovely mate and I can see a shade of pink framing in her cheeks. I hear the Alpha make a sound as if to speak by and by and as I take a gander at him there is a detached look all over, however investigating his eyes you can see bliss. Then, at that point, I glance over to his sibling that has a harsh and to some degree furious look all over.

He approaches me and says, "You better not hurt my child sisters heart. Assuming I at any point discover that you hurt her, I will ensure you get the discipline you merit. Try not to figure I haven't caught wind of your sexual standing." This makes me astounded, I realized that there were bits of hearsay that I would rest around, however I never thought individuals acutally trusted them. Hearing this Derek blasts out chuckling like a lunatic, he begins wheezing and presently I am simply worried for him. Everybody in the room is simply gazing at him like assuming that he were from an alternate planet.

"You really trust those bits of gossip?" Derek says with a powerless voice from all the chuckling. "This most sexual thing this man has done is make-out with a young lady. He is a vir-" before he says whatever else, I cover his mouth with his hand and frown in inconvenience. I glance back at our crowd and see shock in their eyes, particularly Calebs. My mate has clear satisfaction in her eyes, however I can tell that there is a trace of envy in her eyes. Seeing her like this, I advance back to her investigating her eyes and admit, "Indeed, I am a virgin. I have held up for what seems like forever to impart such a private encounter to the one the Goddess has favored me with. What's more I would rehash it in case it implied that it would be you that is my mate." She peers down and becomes flushed a dark red. Endorsement is outlined all around the Alpha, Luna, and her sibling. "I will likewise ensure that she never must have a solitary tragic second for the remainder of her life, if there's anything I can do about it." This causes a grin to develop on my mates face. She has the most excellent grin ever, it could illuminate the haziest of rooms.

"Very much we should simply get the gathering over with the goal that you folks can use whatever remains of the evening to get to know one another." Alpha Emmett says. I gesture in arrangement and we as a whole sit down. The Alpha at the head, Luna at the right, Beta at the left, Gamma sitting close to Luna, Caleb opposite him. I sit close to Gamma Alex and Derek sits infront of me. My little mate planned to sit close to me however I maneuvered her onto my lap and gave her a kiss on the cheek.

This time I actually didn't have a clue about my little mates name, "What's your name holy messenger?"

"Alice," she answered happily.

Alice. I can perceive that this lady will be the passing of me, yet I wouldn't fret.

Chapter 04

"Alpha Jackson, could you specificaly clarify what your concern is? I realize that you are experiencing difficulty with mavericks, expand on that." Alpha Emmett asks utilizing my title which makes me enlarge in pride yet in addition makes me somewhat awkward in light of the fact that he is my future dad in law.

"Well Alpha Emmett, we have been having maverick assaults for as far back as month practically regular. It is unusual in light of the fact that they generally assault in the evening around this time. More often than not the assaults are by gatherings of the greater part twelve of them which confounds me since rebels seldom at any point travel in gatherings. And afterward now and again we will have mavericks going performance. We haven't had one in several days which is the reason I mentioned a gathering." I clarify.

"What have you done to stop the assaults?" Beta Noah inquires.

This time Derek replies, "We have expanded the measure of champions on the lookout, enlisted more fighters, and we have laid out up snares along the boundary however we have just gotten two performances."

"Have you attempted snares from a higher place? Tie a rope low on the ground, when the maverick outings a silver enclosure bound with wolfsbane falls on top. Ezekiel informed me concerning that last week when we were hanging out last week." Alice ringed in. My chest puffs out being prideful that my mate has great technique, yet I immedeately snarled at the way that another male was investing energy with my mate. Alice chuckles and says, "Ezekiel is my mentor, and regardless of whether he has some great looks he is only a companion and is way to old for me. Additionally, your my mate, I will pick you over some other male." This loosens up me, realizing that Ezekiel isn't a danger and that my mate has had preparing. I can hardly wait to see her battle.

"We really haven't contemplated that." I peer down and admonish myself for not doing any better for my pack. "Despite the fact that the rebels have not effectively entered my domain, I actually suck to be the Alpha of the second most remarkable pack." I heard a low snarl realizing it was from my beta and afterward I felt a hand on my shoulder that made flashes shoot all through my body telling me it was my sweet holy messenger.

"Alpha, you ought to at no point ever say those words again. You have been an incredible pioneer and your kin love and regard you." Derek fights. I go to check out him and he is bowing on the floor with his head down. "Derek sit in your seat," I order. He does as he says yet at the same time has his head down.

"He is correct Jackson. I have heard only beneficial things about you. That you are an incredible pioneer and are regarded by your kin. Try not to thrash yourself about this, you began youthful. You are perhaps the most youthful alpha in our hemisphire. Be glad to be as fruitful that you are at this age." Luna Isobel says. I look towards Alice and see a comforting grin all over which make my day.

"We can cooperate in this like a group and these assaults will stop." She guarantees.

Inevitably of more discussion, Alpha Emmett closes the gathering, "Okay, I think I have kept you folks adequately long. Alice how about you take Jackson for supper, you can utilize my card."

"Gracious! I know simply the spot." She stands up and starts to lead me out the entryway until she pauses and glances back at her family. "You better save me some cheesacake or there will be consequences." Once she gives them a hard glare and they all shake their heads in arrangement, she pivots and leads the way.

We stroll for a couple of moments until we are confronting an eatery that is by all accounts asian. We stroll in and are welcomed by little kid that seems, by all accounts, to be in her mid teen years. "Hello Sarah! Is my table accessible?" Alice inquires.

"Welcome Alice. Alpha. You realize your table is continually sitting tight for you. Feel free to I'll tell Ara you are here." Sarah says with a bow and a grin. "Much obliged!" Alice drives me to a little table toward the edge of the café. It is nothing extravagant, indeed it's actual present day and comfortable.

"Heres the menu to take a gander at it. The english adaptation is in the back for the individuals who don't have a clue how to understand korean." Alice clarifies while giving me a menu. "I'm alright bless your heart. I'll simply have whatever you are having," I say and she grins splendidly. No doubt about it, these grins will kill me. A woman in her mid forties approaches us and starts saying stuff that looks bad to me.

(Hey Alice! I see you have a guest, who just happens to be a Alpha. What can I get for you guys?) She says.

Then Alice responds saying,

(Hello Ara. This is my mate Jackson. Can we get two of my regulars please?)

(Oh, how wonderful! I'll get those for you in a few minutes. Congratulations my darling. You better call me every once in a while when you move packs.) The lady says happily. I think she might be Ara.

(Thank you! And I will. How else am I going to practice my korean. You would chase me down with a spatula if I didn't.) Alice laughs. The lady leaves laughing and I am just completely confused right now. Alice sees me and laughs somes more.
"What is going on?" I ask.
"That was Ara, she owns this restaurant and shes been teaching me korean for the past year." She explains and I am just fascinated by my mates knowledge.
"Do you speak any other languages?" I ask and she nods. "I speak english obviously. Fluent spanish, italian, chinese, korean like you just heard, greek, russian, and I think thats it..... Oh wait no, french too." I choke on the water that a waiter hand given to us when we had sat down.
Alice widens her eyes and says, "Oh my Goddess! Are you okay?" I nod my head and wipe the water off my chin with a napkin. "You just surprise me, that's all" I explain.
"Well I hope its in a good way" she says unsure of what to do.
"It is." I assure her and then there she goes again with her smile and lightly blushed cheeks. Our food arrives and we both dig. All I have to say is that it is probably the best thing I have ever eaten. Its sweet but savory at the same time and I can't stop shoving big portions into my mouth. "Slow down, your going to choke if you keep doing that." she laughs out and I obey.

It is currently Sunday morning and the day I get to take my mate home. Recently she showed me around the pack and where she jumps at the chance to eat or invest energy with her companions. The night we met, Friday, we strolled around and conversed with get to know one another more and when we went to the packshouse we shared a cut of cheesecake that she referenced toward the finish of the gathering. Can I simply say, that was the best cheesecake I have at any point tasted. I venture outside the load house with Derek and see Alice and her family remaining in the front yard. Alice is donning high contrast tye-color workout pants, a white shirt, and dark tennis shoes. Her sibling is holding a major bag and a duffle pack. Is that all she is bringing? Typically I would anticipate that girls should bring numerous bags, however I'm not going to say anything.

"Great morning my heavenly messenger, how could you rest?" I kiss her brow and she grins and inquires, "I rested soundly, shouldn't something be said about you?"

"It was OK. In spite of the fact that it would have been exceptional with you close to me." I say with a wink and she becomes flushed. We put everything in the storage compartment and I let her say her farewells.

"Be cautious OK dear. Also put a goddamn sweater on its freezing over here!" Isobel says. "Mother. Quit stressing, I will be fine and I have a sweater in the vehicle in the event that I get cold." Alice consoles.

She embraces everybody and we get in the vehicle. Derek was in one more vehicle that they gave us filled things for the new snares we will set up. When we both lock in I ask her, "Would you say you are prepared?"

"I'm," she answers pleasantly. I grin, start the vehicle and drive out of the Crescent Moon Pack.

Chapter 05

I gradually open my eyes and see my mate. Checking the time, I saw that we have been driving for somewhat more than over two hours. I lower the window and am hit with a whirlwind while contemplating what has occurred for the most recent few days. I have tracked down him. My mate. I actually never figured I would meet my mate like this, yet I guess life has its astonishments. Not going to lie I am very content with this astonishment. Jackson has shown me the most love I might have wished to recieve from a mate, heck, he is absolutley flawless. His highlights are sharp, his skin is smooth and tan appearance how long he spends in the sun. His eyes are almond formed and a wonderful blue blended in with a stunning dark that conflicts into a mix that is memoirizing. Jackson's hair is a characteristic raven dark and how I wish to run my fingers through those perfect locks of his, he fundamentally overshadows me as he is a lot taller, damnation I am the measured of a kid. In any case, his fragrance. Goodness his fragrance, he scents of a sandalwood and citrus, it is absolutley irresistible. I wish to be enveloped by his hug the entire day while never leaving him anytime. I was woken up from my daze when I saw he was saying something,

"Did you rest soundly? You went out cold following a couple of moments," his low delicate voice laughed. I become flushed reasoning how I was unable to rest in light of the fact that Anya needed to be with her mate. I rested soundly like I had said before we left, I simply didn't rest enough.

"Indeed, thank you." I took him in briefly and saw that he look somewhat drained. "Would you like me to dominate? You appear as though you really want a break." He investigates and streaks me a grin. "No it's alright. I got it," he protested, however I could see he needed to acknowledge my proposition.

"Come on. I can see it in your eyes, you really want a break. You didn't rest the previous evening either did you?" I inquired. I keep thinking about whether it very well may be for a similar explanation.

Following a couple of moments he let out a murmur and gestured his head and pulled over. Derek pulled over as well and when Jackson turned a little to unfasten I could see his eyes spacey. I in a split second realized that they were mindlinking. I escaped the vehicle, waved at Derek then, at that point, sat controlling everything of the vehicle. At the point when I close the entryway Jackson asked, "Put your safety belt on."

It makes me snicker and he scowls which makes his temples wrinkle. It was an extremely adorable articulation which made me snicker much stronger. He sulks and shouts, "I'm not kidding! You could get injured."

I look at him without flinching and I can see the worry filling them. I moan and clarify, "Sorry, it's simply that once I shut the entryway you didnt even let me go after the safety belt and your look was delightful."

I watch his glare transform into a grin and we lock eyes for a couple of seconds. We stay like that for some time until we hear a vehicle sound. I put my safety belt on and drive.

"So," Jackson began. "Enlighten me regarding school."

"Well I went to Pre-K, Kindergarten, Middle School, avoided High School and went directly to College. I gratuated top of my group." I expressed while rapidly taking a look of his response. He looked very stunned, yet pride supplanted it. "What might be said about you?" I inquired.

"Same for Pre-K and Kindergarten. But I missed center school, then, at that point, went to High School and College." He expressed gladly.

"Damn." I expressed and he laughed giving me 1,000,000 dollar grin. "Damn for sure." He concurred.

The remainder of the drive resembled that. A lot of inquiries among us to get to know one another.

Following 30 minutes I could feel that the pack was close. Jackson affirmed when he said, "We are nearly there. Only several minutes."

He was correct. After several minutes I could see a portion of his watches wary. They see us and bow allowing us to come in.

"Your pack is delightful," I praise, taking a gander at the trees and wolves on runs.

Perhaps our mate will allow us to go around the pack when we complete the process of getting comfortable. Anya proposed and I concur.

"Much thanks to you. I figure you will like the pack square." Jackson answers.

Before long we are driving and I can see what he was discussing. The pack square was in the pack. It had the emergency clinic, ranchers markets, clothing stores, and so on Driving out of the square I saw their preparation fields and regardless of whether it wasn't generally so large as the one back home, it was as yet great. Jackson saw my advantage and said, "Preparing is held toward the beginning of the day. Here and there the fighters come and train in their available energy, however it isn't needed."

Following the GPS, we end up at this delightful present day frontier home. It's outside was a powdery white and charcol dark illustrating, it was basic yet interesting to the eye. Derek left the vehicle with the snares and my exceptional equiptment they don't know about. I had Ezekiel pack my bows and arrows and shooting hardware. We went into the house and as I strolled up the steps with my gear into what scents like Jackson's room I top around to see the cream hued dividers and splendid light fixture holding tight the roof. It impeccably darkens the room. Be that as it may, what I see next absolutely stuns me. I peered down onto the bed to see a blonde exposed ladies presented on the bed, I am bothered yet not quite so bothered as I hear these words emerge from her mouth, "Jacky child I realized you'd return to me in the long run!" My jaw drops. Were the reports valid? Did this she-wolf truly lay down with my mate, did he deceive me? Was this entire dream materialize dream an untruth... "who are you?" she asks sickened.

"I'm Alice. Jackson's mate." she gazes at me like I developed another head.

"Incomprehensible my Jackson could never pick you over me. I mean have you seen yourself contrasted with me." She waves her give over her exposed body which she presently is covering with a robe. Jackson's robe. Jackson goes into the room as he could most likely hear me conversing with somebody, "Alice what happened?!?!" I gaze at him astounded, would he say he is truly asking what's up when this bare lady was only seconds prior laying on HIS bed?

"This young lady was laying on your bed. Bare." he glances over to see the she-wolf in the room, she is grinning. How amusing.

"Courtney why are the hellfire you here?" his voice was presently blasting through the dividers. I put my hand on his chest, consoling him that he expected to quiet down and that I was fine. His chest brought down and he moaned holding me firmly with his eyes shut.

"Alice, I swear this isn't what you think He says. He twists down to my ear and murmurs, "I'll clarify later."

The young lady that I presently know as Courtney is scowling at me and she sneers, "You must be joking child. It is safe to say that you are actually this dolts mate?"

"First and foremost, she isn't a simpleton. Furthermore, I would reccomend not infuriating me any futher. I have attempted to be great to you since I would rather not be the sort of Alpha that is merciless when slighted. Thirdly, you really want to move past me. We just kissed once. Quite a while back. You are driving me insane gradually and you're not aiding me when you are offending my mate and you future luna." Jackson seethed. I was glad that he was protecting me and he has acknowledged me as his mate and luna.

"Better believe it right! Whats your name bitch?" Courtney addressed. Jackson was going to say reply, yet I put my hand on his arm and addressed myself knowing what she planned to say when I certainly react,

"I go by Alice Clara Blackwood little girl of Emmett and Isobel, Alpha and Luna of the Crescent Moon Pack and mate and luna to Alpha Jackson Dean Tremblay."

Jackson should realize what will happen when he interposes, "Courtney. Try not to do it."

She grins and recits, "I Courtney Williamsburg challenge you Alice Clara Blackwood to a human structure battle for the place of mate and luna to Alpha Jackson Dean Tremblay until accommodation."

Jackson sees me stressed, "Alice-"

Before he can proceed with I say, "I acknowledge."

Chapter 06

I see Jackson run his fingers through his hair and murmuring a "My goodness" faintly. Then, at that point, he keeps on saying, "Courtney. Get out. Presently!" With that Courtney mopes and leaves, righ after she says, "See you in three days time." Challenges were held the following full moon. What's more fortunate for the two of us it was this Wednesday.

At the point when the front entryway shut, Jackson went to sit on the edge of the bed and let out a substantial moan. "I will persuade her to surrender and not battle against you. She's dumb for figuring she can occur as Luna." My head is going around and around. Did I in reality consent to fight somebody I don't have a clue. What assuming that I lose. I'll lose Jackson. I turn upward and our eyes meet, they hold contact for some time before I choose to end the quiet.

"Don't. I can take her. I won't lose without wanting to not lose you. I have been preparing for such a long time to have it be in vain." I essentially snarled out the last part. Assuming I wasn't irate when I saw that she-wolf on the bed, I absolutely am currently.

"Alice I am making an effort not to underrate you and am right behind you on this, however Courtney is probably my best warrior. Allow me to cancel it. I will cause her to submit with my Alpha order and she will cancel the test " I cut him off before he can get done, I definitely know what he is going to say,

"NO. I'm battling her. I couldn't care less assuming she is the 'best' I will prepare hard and battle overall quite well." Jackson is thinking as he takes a gander at the floor for some time. I stroll towards him and he put his arms around my midriff and he puts his head on my mid-region. "I simply don't need you to get injured."

"Relax. I can deal with myself." I say unhesitatingly.

Sooner or later he rises up to leave and opens the entryway before he says, " I'll allow you to settle down. Get to bed early, we train tomorrow at five. Be up."

With my head actually handling all that coincidentally decided, to shower and get into bed. I lay with my eyes shut, its now seven and I'm considering all that could turn out badly.

My considerations are hindered by a thumping at the entryway. "Would i be able to come in...please?", I hear Jackson ask unobtrusively, however enough so that me might hear him. I get up from my position taking the covers off my body and stroll towards the entryway. I turn the handle and open the entryway, Jackson remains there infront of me and very much like whenever I first saw him I am astonished.

He begins to inquire, "Would you like to go for a run and I can show you a greater amount of the pack grounds, before you rest?, he is rearranging to and fro on his feet while taking a gander at the floor. I realize he is concerned and I shouldn't have been so furious and requesting towards him so I say OK, my wolf has been requesting to move the entire day and I can't continue to advise her to stand by.

The breeze feels astounding as it whips through my hide. My paws are beating the ground as I speed past trees. Jackson is right close to me and similarly as I suspected, his wolf is similarly pretty much as beautiful as him. We chose to not allow our wolves to have unlimited authority yet since it has just been a couple of days. We went around the pack edge and were welcomed by a portion of his patrolmen. During that, I was assessing where we could lay out up snares. A couple of miles later we halted at this delightful lake. The sun was practically proceeded to show tints of orange, blue, yellow, and purple. You could see its appearance in the shining water. We choose to move and Jackson goes to take cover behind a tree, I didn't have to. At the point when I previously moved and transformed into my human structure again I was completely dressed. Caleb was really envious as were the wide range of various little guys at school. Jackson left behind the huge oak tree and had a befuddled look all over, however he said nothing. I could have read his minds, perhaps he would ask me later.

"It's delightful isn't it?" He said looking towards the lake. I remained close to him and reacted, "It is."

With a casual murmur he tells me, "Once in a while when I am vexed or sick I come here. I makes them loosen up vibe, I suppose you could say, about it. It causes you to disregard your difficulties and essentially unwind."

"Do you come here frequently?" I inquire. He gestures.

"What are you vexed at this point?" I shoot him another inquiry and he takes a gander at the ground.

"I realize you said that you would be fine, and I realize you can deal with yourself. I can't quit stressing assuming you get injured." I moan and he keeps on saying, "I make an effort not to pass judgment on my pack individuals to an extreme, but rather from what I have seen and heard Courtney can be insane. Once during preparing she was competing with one more of my female heroes, my top female champion to be definite. They would consistently fight together, or more like Courtney needed to beat her and wouldn't stop until she did. Early that day Rhea, the champion, was winning by and by and Courtney saw that and lost it. She moved and began assaulting her, Rhea even submitted to her, however she wouldn't quit assaulting. It took five different heroes to get her to stop. In any case, it was past the point of no return when they did. Fortunately, Rhea didn't bite the dust, yet she has such countless scars. She couldn't prepare as a hero any longer."

"Where is she now?" This totally overwhelmed me. I mean I somewhat realized Courteny was somewhat insane, yet not excessively much.

"She observed her mate when she was all the while recuperating from her wounds. He transfered to our pack to complete his last year of residency at our pack clinic. He was accepeted her as a mate and when he completed she moved to his pack." This alleviated me, I am glad that she observed her mate and he acknowledged her.

"Courtney was next in line to the be top female fighter and nobody battled against her, each female and a few guys aswell fear her." Jackson added. I was beginning to stress assuming she would make a trick like that just to get what she needs, however I wouldn't tell him that. He was at that point stressed, I didn't have to add to that.

"You don't need to stress over me, OK?" I reasured him.

He let out a little chuckle and gazed toward me, "I don't believe that is conceivable." That makes me become flushed hard and peer down at my shoes. I feel him grab hold of my jaw and lift it up with the goal that I investigate his eyes.

"Try not to peer down. You are delightful and I would lie in case I said that I wasn't beginning to succumb to you." He admitted and I can't help but concur.

He peers down to my lips and glances back at my eyes, I do likewise. Then, at that point, we are both left checking out every others lips. We begin to incline in and our lips are not as much as inch separated. In no under a subsequent he shut the distance among us and kissed me passionatly. For my absolute first kiss, it was great. It was loaded up with adoration, care, thus numerous different feelings that etatically wrapped me with an equivalent measure of feeling.

Chapter 07

I woke up to my alert going off and the recollections of the previous evening replaying to me. Alice and I kissed. It was astonishing. I was gradually failing to keep a grip on Jax gradually when it was getting warmed gradually. After the kiss we strolled back to the house and I disclosed to her my past with Courtney. She told me had a thought of what was happening however simply needed my affirmation. She was so understanding with regards to the entire thing, I don't have the foggiest idea what I did to merit such a mate. I stroll into my storeroom and change into some dark b-ball shorts and

I go down the stairs to the kitchen and as of now see my sweet mate in the kitchen tying her shoe bands. She stands upright and glimmers me a grin. Her hair is in a dutch plait, her dark high waisted spandex shorts flaunting her butt and a dark free tank crop top somewhat concealing her dazzling pink games bra. I promise to the Moon Goddess I heard Jax whislte.

"Good day. Are you prepared for preparing?" I ask making a sound as if to speak.

"Good day! Furthermore I am exceptionally energized its been some time since I've prepared." She answers. I was interested how long it has been, "Truly, how long?"

"Two days," she begins, "Last time was the day we met". I was astonished to get directly to the point. On the off chance that I hadn't turned out for two days I would approve of it and assuming not I would simply go for a short run.

Waking up from my contemplations I propose, "Let us go to preparing, will we?"

She gestures her head and we leave the entryway.

———————

"Okay that was three minutes and 21 seconds!" I holler. Alice has competed with a portion of my best champions female and male and she has beaten them all without hardly lifting a finger that is incredible. Alice lets out a hand for my top male fighter.

"Your battling is incredible, yet take a stab at chipping away at your positions and your equilibrium as well." Alice clarifies.

"Much thanks to you, Luna." Stephen somewhat gasped out and added, "You are truly adept at battling, normally just the Gamma, Beta, and Alpha can beat me."

"Discussing Beta, Derek do you mind competing witht Alice?" I ask him. He also has been watching Alice fight with the heroes and like me has been flabbergasted at how great her abilities are.

"Obviously not, I'd be respected as well." He says in a modest voice. "Alice you great?" I ask her and she offers me a go-ahead, "Totally! Gives up Beta Derek."

Derek gets in the competing square and afterward they battle for around ten mintues. Derek got some great hits in however Alice was immaculate.

"I think we have gotten ourselves a fighter as a Luna wouldn't you say, Alpha." Stephan brought up.

"Indeed, you're correct." I admit. "Hello Alice! I need to fight with you!"

She goes to me and I can see shock and shock in her eyes, however it left as speedy as it came, "Game on Alpha." she says in a serious naughty way.

"Here is a contort however," I start and proceed by saying, "We will initially fight in human structure however at that point at whatever point I decide to do as such, we will fight in wolf structure."

"Fine by me." She says with a grin.

"Derek start the stop watch...... Presently!" Just as I said that I thrusted myself to my mate and attempted to carry her down with me, however she got far removed and attempted to trip me yet I moved before she could. I figured since she has battled such a great amount in her human structure I would let her wolf out, so I moved.

She trailed and our wolves were currently confronting each other in guarded positions.

Jax, I want you to quit battling for control. I'm attempting to fight with our mate here, and perceive how solid she is in her wolf structure. I grumble.

Be that as it may, I want to play with mate by the lake like yesterday. He wines. Additionally I would already be able to tell she is solid in this structure check out her.

I was so caught up with attempting to quiet Jax down that I didnt understand Alices' wolf coming at me. At that point it was past the point of no return, I am as of now stuck to the ground, with her on top of me.

Dereks yells out, "Jackson! What happened man? She beat you scarcely following a moment."

Alice gets up movements and I do as well, Derek tossed me a few shorts and I pulled them up. I feign exacerbation at him and clarify, "Jax was giving me trouble and I wasn't focusing."

Alice snickers a bit and it make my day. Her snicker resembles what I really wanted to hear. "I actually need a rematch however," I tell her and she gestures yet blasts out snickering with the others following. "What?!?" I inquire.

"Please accept my apologies. In any case, that was so natural, I didn't need to attempt." She clarifies and I began chuckling as well.

"OK, gives up get changed with the goal that we can discuss those snares." I say and both Alice and Derek follow.

---

After a shower I change into certain pants and a shirt. I hear a thump on my entryway and open it to track down Derek and Alice both dressed and prepared for the gathering. "You prepared man?" Derek inquires.

"Indeed, Let's go." With that we stroll down the road to the packhouse and head into my office where Grayson and a few patrolmen are pausing.

At the point when we as a whole settle down I put down a guide of the entire region and show it to Alice. I point at a specific piece of the guide and say, "This is the place where we get the greater part of our assaults. In any case they are here and here."

"OK. You have added more patrolmen to watch these regions right?" I gesture. "Great, yet don't ensure you remember about the spaces that aren't getting assaulted. Assuming you decline the measure of patrolmen, the rebels will see that in case they are watching which they undoubtedly are. At the point when that happens they will assault those regions and we don't need that. On our run yesterday, I observed where we could set up the snares. For instance, here and here." She discloses as she focuses to the guide.

"In any case, those are the regions that we don't get assaults," Grayson says. "For what reason would we put them there?"

"Indeed, Jackson referenced that you get them pretty regularly, no? To assault so regularly, you should be close. Whats a preferred thought over remaining just external the pack. Assault one side and remain in the other. They would believe that we wouldn't actually look at that side. To get them, you need to think like them." She closed. I checked out the room and saw acknowledgment in their eyes. She was correct, by what other method could they assault so regularly? In case they made want more and forward the Royal patrolmen would have suspected something. The Royal Moon Pack presently known as the Royal Pack is somewhat calm. They just engage with things like wat between packs, any dangers that Alphas trade, or on the other hand assuming a two packs meet up as one. They likewise are the wellspring of our schooling. Assuming a wolf decides to attend a university, they go to the Royal Pack. There are such countless universities to browse.

"Much obliged to you, Alice. The number of traps did your dad pack?" I ask and she answers, "He pressed seven. We can place four around here, since they may be enjoying nature out there yet not to close that they are aware of something occurred. The rest we can put along the remainder of the line and check whether we find anything by any possibility."

"Good thought! Lets head over to our home and begin putting the snares as quickly as time permits." The champions gesture and we head back to my home.

I open the storage compartment of the van and I see the snares, yet what gets my attention the most are these huge cases. "Gracious haha, I'll move these." Alice falters out and it simply tops my interest significantly more.

"What are in those cases?" I ask her.

"Just suplies." She says modestly. I check out her and give her my simply let me know face. "Finnnneeee. They are my firearms, bow and bolt, in addition to my tossing blades."

Somewhere off to the side I see everybody checking out her with shock. My shock was putting it mildly. My mate couldn't just battle and is a decent pioneer, however she can shoot ammunition and bolts and tosses blades.

"You can shoot? Furthermore toss blades?" I inquire. She gestures her head and peers down to her feet. I go to her and lift her jawline so I can look at her without flinching when I tell her, "You astonish me ordinary." She blushes and attempts to keep away from eye to eye connection which makes me laugh.

"I was trusting I could set my objectives up some place, so I could continue to rehearse." She shared. "Obviously, we can set it up in the back with the goal that you don't need to go the entire way to the preparation grounds." I say.

"Much thanks to you." She reacts. "Anything for my mate." I murmur in her ear and can feel her shiver against me.

Chapter 08

It is presently one PM on Wednesday. It is the day of the test and the Luna Ceremony. The fate of this pack relies upon Alice and Courtney now. I heard that Courtney has been preparing extra hard. I'm sure Alice will dominate this game, however I'm worried about the possibility that that Courtney may pull something. Like two days prior we began our day via preparing and going over the how to assemble the snares and conceal them. Today the patrolmen simply need to put the last snare close to the rebels hideaway outside the eastern side of the pack. Recently we observed a lot of old fire pits and dead creatures like deer, squirrel, and hares. During this brief time frame, Alice and I have been going out and falling further enamored constantly. I'm in my office going over some pack issues and I conclude that I will go visit Alice. She referenced she was going to rehearse with her bow. I return home and stroll to the terrace and see her holding her bow up to the objective that is set on an oak tree. I stop when I'm a couple of feet away and stop to watch her. She takes in a full breath and taps her foot on what resembles a romote. Every one of the unexpected focuses of different sizes and distances are flying throught the trees. Quickly she shoots each moving and still objective without thinking twice. There were three targets left swinging around like monkeys, she takes one huge bolt, brings it back and shoots. The bolt was penetrating through the center of every one of the three targets.

"How would you figure out how to look so effortless while doing risky things?" I ask her and she laughs

"I can show improvement over that, I was simply being lethargic today."

"I don't question it." I answer.

"Jackson?" I murmur a yes. "May I ask what befell your folks? We haven't actually contacted that subject and there isn't anything in the house that infers that they were even separated of your life."

I murmur, "My folks passed on several months prior to I turned eighteen in a fender bender. Well not actually an auto collision but rather, they were en route to visit the Full Moon Pack when their vehicle detonated on non-guaranteed land. I was as yet in college so I was unable to dominate unexpectedly early so his Beta was in control. Also my dad never truly encouraged me how to finish my Alpha obligations... that is the reason we are deficient. I don't have the foggiest idea how we are even the second most grounded pack on the planet."

She puts a hand on my shoulder and tells me, "I'm exceptionally sorry Jackson. I can't start to envision how agonizing that probably felt like. I will consistently be hanging around for you, mate or not."

"Much obliged to you, Alice." I say and kiss her on the lips. She kisses me back and we stay like this for a couple of moments.

"We ought to get inside so you can eat and rest for this evening." I remind her breaking our kiss.

"You're correct. I'm somewhat restless to be straightforward." She admits.

"Try not to be. I know I'm not. You don't have anything to stress over. I have confidence in you and realize you can beat her." I lie to her. I realize she can beat Courtney obviously, yet I am probably multiple times more restless than she is. However, i can't tell her that. I must be solid for her.

We head inside and we have extras from the previous evening. While I eat I can't quit checking out her. She is so wonderful and kind and the closest friend of all time. She turns upward from her serving of mixed greens at me and asks with a significant piece of lettuce, "What?"

She was so charming and I needed to save this second to me.

"Nothing. You're not kidding." She becomes flushed hard which makes me need to kiss her.

After we eat I lead her to her room and say, "All things considered, I should pass on you to rest."

I was going to leave when she snatches my wrist and says, "Pause. Would you be able to remain with me?"

"Is it true that you are certain? I would rather not cause you to feel awkward." I tell her.

She shakes her head, "No, that wouldn't be imaginable. I truly need you to remain with me."

I gesture my head and stroll into the room just after her. She strolls into the wardrobe and comes out with some shorts and a loose shirt. Her hair is placed into an untidy bun and she moves into the fronts of the bed. I move in and make a point to maintain some separation however be pretty much as close as could be expected. She goes to confront me and cuddles into me. Jax was attempting to push foward and take control so he could be with his mate.

"Much thanks to you." I hear her sweet voice say.

"For what?" I inquire.

"Everything." Saying that I felt her pulse consistent, connoting that she nodded off.

"I ought to thank you." I murmur to her and give her a kiss on the highest point of her head. Following a couple of moments, I nodded off to the rhythym of my mates heartbeat.

--------------------------

My alert is blasting and I awaken to see my mates eyes ripple open.

"It's time isn't it?" She asks with a moan. I gesture my head and kiss her full lips. We get up and I tell her, "Relax, you got this. I'll sit tight for you down steps."

To begin with, I go to my room and change into a dark suit for the Luna Ceremony. I had Grayson plan it with nuteral colors so Courtney wouldn't overplay it. After the match, the cereommy will be held behind the packhouse. There will be the customary bloodpromise and stamping. On the off chance that Courtney loses, she will be kicked out of the pack. She isn't permitted to join one more pack since she tested and sabotaged her chiefs. I get done with getting dressed and head down to the family room where Derek and Grayson are pausing.

"Great evening Alpha, everything for the test and Luna Ceremony is prepared." Grayson claims.

"Try not to stress Alpha, Im sure our actual Luna will dominate this game." Derek tolls in.

I gesture in appreciation and think back when I hear strides descending the steps. Alice catches high waisted dark stockings, dull dim fitted games crop top, dark Nike running shoes, and her hair was up in a high pig tail with a meager dark headband.

"I'm prepared." She breathes out.

"OK. We should go."

We head to the preparation gorunds where there is a fighting ring and lines of seats for the pack individuals. It seems as though there will be a MMA battle. Practically every one of the seats are full, everyone holding on to see who their Luna will be. I had been acquainting Alice with a few pack individuals all through these beyond couple of days. I would get private mindlinks from them saying that they love her and that they hope everything turns out great for her of karma.

After some trusting that the moon will ascend and pack part to arive the time had come to start. I stroll to the focal point of the ring and start the opening.

"Hi pack individuals!" I blast out. "As you most likely are aware your top female fighter Miss Courtney Jennings tested my mate and genuine luna, Alice Clara Blackwood. She has provoked her to a human duel to accommodation. Courtney and Alice, if it's not too much trouble, venture into the ring." I call out. The two of them stroll into the ring. Alice looks quiet and Courtney is attempting to turn me on by pushing her breats up that are now jumping out of her extra-little games bra. I feign exacerbation and check out the group.

"With respect to rules... any conning that incorporates any weapons like blades, edges, and so forth will discualify the contender." I think back to Alice and Courtney. "Do you undersatnd or do you really want me to explain anything?"

"I comprehend." They both state.

COURTNEY'S POV

That bitch. How could she think that she was going to take my alpha away from me. Everyone in the pack knows that he belongs to me. She can't just walk in and pretend she is his mate. And how does he even like her she isnt even that attractive. Ever since she got here she has been acting like miss perfect. I've heard people talk about her time in the Cresecent Moon Pack and how she was trained by a soldier that was from the Royal Pack, but that doesn't scare me. She may beat me in this challenge but I have something that little miss perfect doesn't.

ALICE'S POV

Having Jackson sleep with me really helped my nerves. Sure I was confident in myself, but never in my life would I have thought that I would have to do this. I feel a little bad because if she loses she will mostly become rouge. Very few people manage to become a lone wolf especially if they were kicked out. But that isnt going to stop me from fighting for my true mate. I've waited for so long to just simply give up.
"Then...... You may begin!" Jackson orded.
Courtney comes charging foward and tries to punch me but I manage to dodge her hit. I go for a punch in the lower stomach but she gets a hold of my arm and twists it, which makes it hurt like a bitch. Thats why I'm thankful for the quick healing a werewolf gets. I manage to kick her down so that I would be on top of her. I start to punch her on the jaw which starts to knock her out little by little. But something was wrong. This was too easy. She's the top female warrior, she should be better than this. And I was right. Right before I could punch her once more, I felt a sharp burning stab on my side and a hard blow to my jaw. And I was knocked out. Silver and wolfsbane, of course. She knew she wouldn't have won so she came prepared. This combination is deadly, I knew what was coming for me, but there was something else. Something

that was aliving. I just a few seconds I opened my eyes to see
Courtney about to give me another blow. Her fist was an inch
away but I stopped it, twisted it, and head bumped her to so
that she could get off of me. She was shocked but I don't
blame cause I am too. I'm supposed to be dead or at least
severely infected. But I'm mad. She cheated. I won't show her
anymore mercy. I get up and kick her in the stomach which
make her bend over in pain. I go behind her and kick her in
the back of her head and she falls to the ground. I get on her
back and pick up her head by the front of her neck causing
her to struggle breathing. She was crying and begging me to
let go. And thats when I heard his voice.
"The winner is... Alice!"
I let her go and she was heaving and gasping for air. I get up
and start walking out of the ring but stumble every once and
a while. Jackson notices and starts walking quickly towards
me.
"Are you okay?" I nod in response but then I feel another
sharp stab of pain where Courtney stabbed me. I put pressure
on it with my hand, but Jackson moves it to see what
happened. He growls loudly and and shifts to his wolf form
and runs back to the ring. Derek runs towards me and guides
me to the the packs clinic where me meet the doctor.
"Luna, what happened?" Dr. Smith asks. "Courtney stabbed
me with a sliver knife laced with wolfsbane during the
match." I replied.
He led me to a bed and checked out my wound. It had a burn
around but it looked nearly healed.
"Luna, I dont know how you survived this. You should be
dead, how did you survive?"
"I have no idea." I tell him.
Just then the door slams open and in walks Jackson with
extremely messy hair and a pair of jeans and a t-shirt, since
his suit was destroyed when he shifted.
"Alpha." Both Derek and Dr. Smith say together while bowing
their heads. Jackson ignores them and comes straight to me.
He checks my wound and then hugs me, pushing me into his

chest and inhaling my scent which seems to calm him down a bit.

"How is she?" His rough voice says.

"She is better than any other person I've seen with this type of wound, especially since it is very recent. But she still needs some rest." Dr. Smith replies.

"Derek," Jackson looks at him. "Send eveyone home, we will be canceling the Luna Ceremony tonight."

"What!?" I yell. "No. We will not be doing that." Jackson looks at me in disbelief.

"I've come a long way to have to wait a month more. Derek?"

"Yes Luna?" He turns to look at me.

"Tell the people we will take a little longer than expected but will be there as soon as possible."

"Of course, Luna." And he heads out the door.

"Alice, what are you doing? You should be resting." Jackson worries.

"Jackson, Dr. Smith said I'm okay. Just give me some pain killers and I'm good. Plus, we have a Luna Ceremony to get to."

"Are you sure? We don't have to do it tonight."

"Yes we do. Now let's go." He hesitantely nods and we walk out together after Dr. Smith stitches me up and gave me the pain killers.

We walked up to his house and went to our rooms. When I went in, there was a beautiful, floor-length white satin dress with a deep v and spaghetti straps. On the floor there was a pair of white shoes with a silver point. I took a quick shower and got dressed. I took two strands of hair and tied them to the back. Then I applied a little bit of make-up. Once I finished making the finishing touches I went down to find Greyson waiting for me on the living roomm?

"Luna. Are you okay?" He starts.

"Yes, thank you." He nods and opens the front door for me. He leads me to the car and we head to the packhouse where the Ceremony is going to be held. Greyson told me that Jackson had left a few minutes beofre me because due to tradition the Alpha couldn't see his Luna in her dress before the Ceremony. Its quite similar to the humans. They have the tradition that the groom couldn't see the bride at all the day they are to be wed. We arrive to the packhouse and Greyson opens the door and leads me to where I would enter when my name is called.

"Good luck Luna." He said before joining the other pack members.

I wait a few minutes and everything starts to quite down. "Packmembers!" Jacksons voice begins. "This night, under the full moon we will be welcoming a new member to this pack. My mate and Luna." Everyone started whistling and rejoycing. "Now, may Alice Clara Blackwood please come out?" Right then I walked out from the side and was faced with a huge crowd with lots of gasps. I continued walking towards Jackson and felt everyones eyes on me. I was used to be in crowds but that didn't stop me from being nervous. I meet Jackson on the mini stage and he starts again, "Alice. Do you promise to take care of the pack and complete your duties as your position of Luna?"

"I do."

"Do you promise to stay loyal to your pack no matter what?"

"I do."

"Now lastly, Do you promise to love and protect this pack for as long as the moon shines on us?"

I take a deep breath. "I do."

Jackson nods at Derek, who brings over a small box. He opens it and it reveals a blade. But its not any blade, its the blade that only works under the moon. Jackson takes the blade and cuts his palm and does the same to mine. He binds them together and says, "Then Alice, Welcome to the Blood Moon Pack." All of the sudden I felt a rush in my mind that meant that my mindlink was now connected to the Blood Moon Pack. Everyone linking me and saying 'Welcome'.

"Now to complete this proccess and for you to recieve your title we fnish with marking each other." I look at Jackson and nod. Marking is a very vital part for mates. It signifies that they have found their soulmate and are 'owned' by each other. It may sound foolish to some but it is quite beautiful if you really understand what its like. Jackson leans into my necks and kisses the spot where he is going to mark me, which makes me gasp. Then all of the sudden is canines are in my neck, making me let out a quite moan. After a few seconds, he pulls out but stays bent over so that I could reach his neck. I wanted to tease him a little so licked the spot on his neck making him grunt. and slightly jump. He did not expect that at all.

"One day, I will get payback." He whispered in my ear. And with that I sunk my teeth in his neck.

After everyone had stopped by us to welcome me and congratulate us, we decided to go home.

When we got home we were very tired and we went straight to bed. Tonight we both decided that we would sleep together in his room and move all my things to his closet the next morning. We setteled in the bed and were out.

I start waking up to the sound of someone knocking on the door, I quickly get up and go to my room to get a robe. Once I get out of my room Jackson is at the doorway of his or our room. The knocking is harder so we gead downstairs together. I open the front door to see Dr. Smith with a slightly worried and confused face.

"Dr. Smith, whats wrong?" I ask.

"Luna, who are you?"

Chapter 10

I was confused. What did he mean?

Jackson hearing my thoughts asks, "Dr. Smith, what are you talking about? This is your Luna."

"Yes Alpha, I know. But it seems that there is more to our Luna than what we know."

"Alice , my angel, what is he talking about?"

"I have no idea. Dr. Smith, what ARE you talking about."

"The blade that Courtney used was silver and it was laced with silver. As you both know, that is a deadly mix for our kind. But forntuantely, Luna is still with us."
"What are you trying to say?" Jackson asked starting to get a little stressed and confused. I held his hand so that he would calm down and he looked down at me feeling the sparks that appear when our skin makes contact.
"What I'm saying Alpha is that after some research, it appears that the Luna has some power that only one family holds."
"The Blackwoods?" I ask since that is the name of my family.
"No Luna. The Ashfords.... The Royal family."
"What?" I whispered. I was in utter shock. "How is that possible? I lived in the Cresecent Moon Pack my whole life."
"That I cannot answer, Luna. That is something you need to ask Alpha and Luna Blackwood." Dr. Smith said and with a bow he left.
"Jackson, I need to go back. I need answers." I was telling him frantically while walking towards my room to pack some clothes.
Following me he responds, "Okay, but I am coming with you."
"What about the pack?"
"Derek will be in charge he already knows."
"Thank you Jackson."
He walks towards me while I close my bag and kisses me on the forehead and hugs me. It calms me down and I go help him pack a bag.
Once we finished we walked to his black pickup and drove off. After a few hours later, we arrived to our pack and the wariors let us pass through. We pulled up to the pack house, where my father or whoever he is, would most likely be. I walked in and found my so called "family" talking about some pack I felt . They looked up and you could see the shock in their faces.
"Alice dear, what a surprise! Why didn't you tell us you were coming? I would have made some arrangements for you and your mate." Mom starts and she then looks at me up and down and stares down where my neck and shoulder meet.

"Oh Goddess! You are marked, congratualations honey." She starts walking towards me, opening her arms for a hug, but I stop her. Now was not the time for formalities.

"Whats wrong?" She asks with a worried face.

"I want to know the truth." I state.

My father chimes in asking, "The truth about what?"

"My real family."

"Alice, what are you talking about? We are your family." Caleb says. "Right mom, dad?" He looks back at them. It was clear that he didn't know. But my parents did. They looked at him with some sadness and and looked back at me.

"We are so sorry Alice. We can explain." Dad confesses.

"What is going on? What did you do to my sister?" Caleb gets up angrily and walks towards my mate with clenched fists who was standing quietly behind me.

I pushed him back and scolded, "DO NOT TOUCH MY MATE!" Anya was coming out, she felt very protective of her mate. Her voice was loud and held much more power than an Alpha's.

Caleb backed away, he could feel her power and he kneeled and exposed his neck in submission. So did my parents. Seeing them doing this did not feel normal, it was overwhelming and I couldn't process what was going on. I started hyperventilating and crying, it was too much.

I felt his arms around waist and slowly I started to steady my breathing but I was still crying a little. He turned me around and and hugged me tightly, it calmed me down and I was glad that Jackson came with me.

"Let's go to our room." He whispered in my ear and I nodded. I'll have to speak with them, right now I want to spend time with my mate.

"We can talk later, during dinner maybe. If that's alright." Jackson told my family, he must have been lsitening to my thoughts.

Caleb and my parents got up and stood straight nodding their heads. Jackson and I walked out and I could hear Caleb asking my parents what was going on. We entered our room where our bags were. We didn't bother changing our clothes and went to sleep.

A few hours later I woke up to my mates face buried in my neck. It was so cute, his lips were pouting and I just wanted to kiss them. Just then his head came up and he kissed me on the lips. His lips were so soft I just wanted to kiss them all day.

"We can do that if you want," he said once again listening to my thoughts.

"I wish we could, but we have to go speak with my parents." I replied.

"We do," He checked his phone and continued, "its four pm, do you want to do anything before dinner?"

"Can we go see Ezekiel? I kinda wanna train a little and he trains 24/7."

"Of course, lets get changed."

We both changed into our workout clothes and headed to the training fields. On our way there, I saw all of my latest pack members. When we arrived at the gym I saw Ezekiels car and another familiar car but couldn't quite remember where I have seen it before. We parked the car and went inside to find Ezekiel training another female and thats when I figured out who it was.

"CYNTHIA!?!?!??!" I yell.

The fit red headed girl that stands at 5'5 turns around and yells back, "ALICE!?!?"

"Oh my goddess!" I run towards her and give her a big hug which she gives back.

"When did you come back from nursing school?" I ask.

"Just yesterday morning. When were you going to tell me you had found your mate and moved away?"

"It all happened so fast i totally forgot." I replied. Just then I heard two male voices clear their throats.

I turned to Jackson and explained, "Cynthia is Ezekiels niece and my best friend. She is a year older and we went to school together, but she had stayed longer to attend to nursing school." Then I turned to Cynthia and introduced her to my

mate, "Cynthia, this is my mate Jackson. He is the Alpha of the
Blood Moon Pack. We met last Friday."
"It's nice to meet you." Jackson said and shook her hand.
"Likewise." She replied.
"Ezekiel." I said
"Yes Alice?"
"I was wondering if Jackson and I could go to the shooting
range downstairs and practice."
"Of course, it's all set up so you don't have to worry about
that."
"Great, I'll see you guys later!"
---------------------------
After I took Jackson to practice some shooting with all types
of guns and rifles, we said our goodbyes to Ezekiel and
Cynthia and headed to the packhouse to get ready for
dinner. We both took a quick shower and changed into casual
clothes. On our way to the dinning room, I sensened more
people apart from my family. How many people knew about
my real family? As we entered, there was my mother, father,
Caleb, Beta Noah, Gamma Alex, and most importantly Ezekiel.
We sat down and the chefs including Sofie entered with our
food.
"Tonight we have prepared Alices favorite Italian dish.
Chicken Fettucini Alfredo served with Pasta e Fagioli. And
Ezekiels Greek Salad."
"Thank you Sophie, I have missed your cooking for sure."
"It's good to see you dear. Enjoy!" She said as she and the
other chefs left.
"Let's start from the begining shall we?" My father said.
"We shall." I said.
"After we had your brother, we failed to concieve another
child. And we were so happy that we had the chance to have
you. It is true, you are not our biological daughter, but we feel
as if you were. It was all planned since the Queen discovered
she was pregnant. Except nobody knew except for those who
worked in the castle and they swore to secrecy." He started
"Why was she a secret?" Jackson asked.

"When the King and Queen had marked and mated each other they had started to recieve anonymous threats that all of their children would be brutally killed one by one. That one mating resulted in you, Alice, and they were so happy to have you but they knew that if they kept you in the palace someone might take you away regardless of the amount of security put on you. They didn't know who they could trust anymore. That is when Isobel had recieved a letter from the Queen asking her for a favor. The Queen was to rule from the inside of the palace making everyone on the outside believe that she was terribly sick. Isobel was to pretend that she was pregnant and Dr. Miller who has retired and moved was to pretend to be her private physician. They would send letters to eachother back and forth giving each other updates. After nine months the Queen gave birth and sent Ezekiel sneak out and bring you to us. The Queen stayed isolated for a few more months because she didn't want to make anyone suspicious of her."
"Why didn't they keep in contact?" I ask with tears in my eyes.
"They knew that if they did, they would want to bring you back, they couldn't risk that. But in our agreement we were to bring you back to the palace once you had marked and mated with your other half." My mother continued.
"Is that why you sniffed me when I came into Dads office this morning?" She looked down and nodded.
"Let's eat!" I changed the subject. We all began eating in a uncomfotable silence. It was slowly starting to make sense, how I could beat almost everyone one in the pack, but now I'm sure that if I tried, I could beat my dad making me being able to beat everyone in this pack.
After we finished eating dessert Jackson and I agreed to go up stairs and call it a night. Before we left the dinning room, I turned around and told them, "We will leave for the palace tommorow morning at dawn mated or not."
My parents nodded in agreement and so did Ezekiel.

Before we headed up the stairs I remembered that I had forgotten to bring my cello. "Wait for me in our room, I'll be right there in a sec." I told Jackson.

"Okay. See you in a bit." He kissed me and went up.

I went down to the basement where there was a small music room where I would stash all of favorite albums and records. In the corner lied my cello. It's been a while since I played, I think its been a month. I took the strap and put it over my shoulder. I entered the room and Jackson changed into his sleeping shorts and had lied a pair of my own pajamas on the bed. Once I changed I took my cello out, tuned it, and started playing by the window. The moonlight shining brightly into our room and as our only source of light it lit up the room pretty well. I started playing the "Four Seasons" by Vivialdi. It was one of the most challenging pieces I have ever learned. I closed my eyes, pressed my bow against the strings and started playing. Playing the cello always calmed Anya and during this time she has been a little stressed.

Sometime later once I finished play the last season, Winter, I opened my eyes seeing Jackson sitting in the seat in front of me. He had a big smile on his face and said, "You play beautifully. No wonder you have such grace when you shoot and fight."

I giggled, "Thank you, I'm glad you liked it."

"I loved it, let's go to bed." He said and I coulnd't wait to go back to sleep.

-------------------------

I woke up to an empty bed but saw the bathroom light on and that Jackson was showering. I got up and took out my outfit for today, black dress pants with a light blue grey turtle neck. I also picked out my black stiletto heels and brought my black blazer just in case I get cold. To top it all off I picked out a silver necklace with a small cresent moon Cynthia got me for my sixteenth birthday, so that if I ever found my mate before she did I would never forget her. I really hope she finds her mate soon. Jackson walked out of the bathroom with a towel around his waist and hist chest and hair had water slowly falling down. It was getting really hot in here. Walking towards me, he chuckled and gave me a kiss on the forehead. "Good morning angel, I hope you slept well."

"I did, thanks. What about you?" I asked as he walked into the closet to change.

"I always do when I'm with you." His reply made me blush a deep red.

"Ok well, I'm going to hop in the shower real quick." I said and ran into the bathroom. That man does things to me and he knows it.

After my shower, I changed and we headed downstairs to the kitchen. I made us some Taylor Ham, Egg, and Cheese Bagels and a cup of orange juice for each of us. Once we ate, we brushed our teeth and headed to my parents house. My parents, Ezekiel, and Cynthia were standing outside.

As I got out of the car I asked, "Cynthia, are you coming with us?"

"I am, my uncle told me everything after the dinner. Are you okay?"

"I will be once I meet my real parents."

"Oh goddess. I can't believe your a princess."

"Oh please don't remind me."

"Of course..... your higness." She teased and started laughing and so did I.

I turned to everyone else and said, "We will first drive up to my new pack to settle some current pack business with the beta and after that we will head straight to the Royal Pack."

"You brother is going to stay with Fiona and his pups, so let's head out." My father adds.

"Ok. Let's go." Jackson and I go in his car, my parents in theirs and Cynthia and Ezekiel go in his.

Just as we left the pack territory I was hit with the realization that I had forgotten my cello in our room.

*Actually, I put it in the trunk while you were making breakfast.* Jackson mindlinked me.

"Really!?!? Thank you so much." I squeled.

He chuckled and continued driving. Three hours later we arrived to our packhouse where Derek was waiting for us. Everyone else parked behind us but waited in their cars. Derek came out of the house and greeted us, but before we could greet him back, I heard a female growl out, "MINE!"
I turn to see Cynthia run towards Derek and he catches her and takes in her scent. We let them stay like that for a while but then have them come inside to finish our pack business. Once its setteled me and Jackson start to get up, but before we leave I tell Cynthia, "Hey Cynth, stay here with Derek and get to know him and your future pack."
"Thanks Ally, good luck."
"Thanks, see you soon."
-----------------------------------

We arrived at the Royal Pack and headed to the Palace. Other than Unisversities the Royal Pack also consists of many national and international businesses and there is a suburban area near by for the member of the Royal Pack. The Palace gates opened and we drive up to a beautiful stone castle. It was gigantic with big windows and balconies. Outside their was a beautiful big pond and garden. All types of trees surronding everything, provding just enough shade.
We parked our cars in the front by a fountain and were guided to the throne room. We went inside and it was huge. With large windows allowing the natural light come in. The golden chandaliers hanging were the size of my bed. The pillars were so tall, whoever designed this room was surely talented. I was so distracted with taking in the beauty of the room, I didn't realize someone else entered the room.
When I heard footsteps come towards me I looked to see two adults in their late 40s staring at me with wonder, "Alice, is that you?"

Chapter 11

"Alice?" The voice said.
I turn around to find a couple around the same age as my parents. The man was a few inches taller than Jackson and

had dirty blonde hair with hazel eyes. The woman looked exactly like me but older, dark hazlenut hair with deep blue eyes like the ocean. I walk towards them and hold both of their hands. All of the sudden, I am hit with a bunch of memories of when my real mother was pregnant with me. I saw exactly what my parents told me: the threats, the conversations between mothers, my actual birth, and my parents sending me away with Ezekiel to the Crescent Moon Pack where I grew up.

I gasp and open my eyes to eveyones eyes on me, I was laying on the floor and was starting to get a headache. Everyones gives a sigh of relief and Jackson leans down to help me up, "Give me your hand angel."

I give him my hand and he pulls me up. My mom, or Isobel comes to me with a glass of water. I drink the water and the King or my real father says, "Are you alright?"

"Yes." I answer.

The Queen comes to me and gives me a big hug, "Oh Alice! It is so good to see you, I love you so much. I am so sorry that your father and I couldnt have been there all these years."

I was in so much shock and Anya was going crazy as well. She was reconizing their their scents and their aura. I started tearing up and gave both of my birth parents a hug, their scents invading my nostrils, pinewood and vanilla. Due to their mating, their scents mix together. The physical contact with the two of them created a new bond between me, Anya, them and their wolves. My father named Luka, his wolf is called Lane. My mother named Sienna, her wolf is called Sawyer. After staying in the same position for a while, we come apart and Luka says, "We haven't had breakfast yet, would you all like to join us for brunch?"

"Of course!" I responded.

We were led to the dinning hall and we all sat down to eat. The maids walked in carrying trayfulls of food. From various fruits to all types of breakfast meats like ham and bacon. They also brought in different beverage options like juices, teas, coffee and more. We all dove in and started eating and catching up. We talked about my childhood, how Ezekiel had trained me, me going to university and meeting Jackson. My father was very skeptical for a while, but after getting to know him more he warmed up to him. But my mother, one look and she was in love. It was as if she just found her own mate, it was funny.

Jackson and I decided to stay for a week or two but my non biological parents had to go back and take care of the pack. Ezekiel stayed because he wants to be with Cynthia and I. Derek and Grayson are staying in charge of the Blood Moon Pack while we are here.

For the two weeks that we are staying, Jackson and I are going to go run around the Palace and maybe even go visit our old schools and other places we used to go to. We had all planned a date for each day of our stay.

-------------------------------------

It is our last day and we had gone on our moring run around the forests near the palace. Then we went to the movie theater which was on the other side of the Royal Moon Pack which took a few hours to get there.

We get to back to the palace and have dinner with my parents and Ezekiel. Then we go to our room and take a relaxing bath and get ready for bed.

Laying on the bed, Jackson finishes using the bathroom and comes out to lay next to me. By this time it was dark and a little of the moonlight was coming into the room.

"I love you." I blurt out. Jackson turns around and gives me a huge smile.

"Really?"

"Yes, really. I have been wanting to tell you for a while actually."

"I'm glad because I love you too my angel." This makes me smile as well and I lean in for a long passionate kiss. The kiss was starting to get heated and we were all over each other. I started taking his shirt off and took off mine. All of the sudden Jackson stopped and looked me in the eyes.

"Are you sure you want to do this?" He asks, awaiting an honest reponse.

I nod my head and say, "Yes."

"Are you absolutely sure? I don't want to do anything you are not ready for."

"Just shut up and makde love to me Jackson." I declare looking him straight in the eyes like he did me.

His eyes turned as dark as night and you could tell that Jax was sharing control with him. He started kissing me again and the rest of the night was a magical experience.

Chapter 12

I wake up to Jacksons soft snoring. He is so adorable when he sleeps, his lips pout a little and it makes me want to kiss him all day. Now, when mates mark eachother they can read each others minds, but when they mate they can go into their minds and see what they are dreaming. And if your bond is very strong and powerful you can see from your mates perspective. I can feel Anya itching me to see what he was dreaming. I am quite curious myself and focus on his sleeping face and enter his mind.

He was standing in the garden here at the palace watching something with a huge grin on his face. I turn to the direction of where he is looking and I see two little kids, twins, around the age of 5 running around and having fun. They were so cute and looked exactly like us, its as if someone just pressed the copy and paste button.

I hear a womans voice come towards my direction say, "Adeline! Killian! Get ready for our evening run at the treeline!"

"Yes mommy," the twins said in unison and ran off. The woman who called to them was me. Future me was walking towards Jackson with a small smile on her face. When she reached him, she wrapped her arms around his neck while he wrapped his around her waist and they kissed passionately on the lips.

"Are you ready, my angel?" Jackson asks.

"Always." She respond.

"Lets go." He says back and they both walk towards the treeline shifting in the proccess.

It was the end of the dream and Jacksons opened eyes are looking straight into mine.

"Good morning handsome." I smiled cheekly.

"Good morning beautiful." He smiles back and gives me a peck on the lips. "Do you want to go eat breakfast?"

"Breakfast sounds really good right now." I giggled out.

----------------------------------

We changed into casual but comfortable clothes since we are leaving an hour after breakfast.

Walking into the dinning room, I see both Sienna and Luka sniff the air and grin in excitement. Sienna gets up and runs towards me and gives me the tightest hug ever.

"Congratualations Alice! Oh Luka, I can't wait to see little pups running around the palace!"

"You and me both, darling." He says as he comes foward and gives me a hug aswell. When he walks back to his seat he adds, "And when their time comes they will be great leaders."

"Speaking of leaders," I start. "What was the plan once I was brought here after being marked and mated to my mate?" I ask Luka.

"Well, your mother and I planned on coming out with your true story to the public and retire a few weeks after you and your mate would settle down here. But Jackson is an Alpha, so that does change things a little."

"How so?" Jackson chimes in.

"Well we don't expect you to just stop ruling your pack and come rule ours. As Alpha of the Blood Moon Pack it makes things easier for the change. Once you are both crowned King and Queen both packs will conjoin and form one. The new bigger pack will have to stay with the name of the Royal Moon Pack but it would be like adding a very large group of people to your pack at once. It may seem very diifucult to understand but it will make sense in the moment."

Jackson and I nod our heads in understandment and continue eating. After a few minutes we finish and head back to our room to pack whats left to go back home.

----------------------------------

Jackson shuts the storage compartment of the vehicle where our baggage is securely kept. I go to say my farewells and get in the vehicle and before long Jackson follows. He gets the motor and drives going. Inevitably I begin feeling restless, I feel like something downright awful will occur. Jackson more likely than not been paying attention to my contemplations since he inquires as to whether I need him to stop the vehicle so I can get some natural air which I consent to. He halted before a huge cleaning a couple of miles up from the castle and not to far away from the line. I escaped the vehicle and took in a couple of full breaths yet nothing was working. On the off chance that anything I was getting more restless and Anya was on guard. I began sniffing the air the extent that my noses could deal with. Furthermore that is the point at which I smelled it. "Rebels." I murmured out. Jackson most certainly heard me on the grounds that once the word avoided my mouth he immediately got with regard to the vehicle and remained adjacent to me in an exceptionally defensive position. The terrible smell was coming from the clearing and I strart to search for any development, however come up short. This time I center around a large portion of my faculties, my touch, hearing, sight, and smell.

"Theres around a few handfuls out there." I tell Jackson pointing straight in front of us. They were around 3 miles away yet in wolf structure that isn't anything.

"How could they traverse the gatekeepers at the line?" I truly had no clue about how, every watchman was prepared to be to take on no less than 6 mavericks all at once. However at that point I recollect the alternate way that no watchman ensures. The old way that Ezekiels mate took and was killed by nonother than rebels. Jackson holds my hand and gives me a gesture letting me know he heard.

I rapidly mind interface Sienna, Sienna! There are rebels at the cleaning a couple of miles up from the castle! There are around 3 many them!

She reacts not even a large portion of a second after the fact, We are sending fortifications at this moment! Luka and I are coming aswell.

I could hear many watchmen and heroes coming our however they wouldn't have been here on time since those rebels began running towards us. Jackson and I shift and run towards them. Fortunately the fortifications arrived exactly when we are a couple of feet from the mavericks. I propel myself off the ground and hop on top of a rebel and chomp his neck watching his life leave his eyes. Ezekiel was here with us however he left recently a couple of hours before breakfast. I check out the scene before me, champions and rebels battling each other left and right. I spot Jacksons wolf, Jax polish off a rebel. He looks towards me send a 'I'm alright' look. That is until he runs towards me and pushes me far removed when he collides with a maverick. The maverick nibbles on Jaxs shoulder and he lets out a little cry, a physical issue like that can recuperate rapidly for an alpha, however it actually harms like a bitch. I get up and run towards the maverick that tore into him and I bit his side. Jax before long got up as well and the two of us were gnawing and pawing at maverick passing on it to bite the dust.

Jax runs off to help a youthful champion who is warding off about six rebels. One more about six come at me, yet I am ready. I kick, paw, and snap at all of them, yet that doesn't stop them. Sure I was prepared by awesome, everything going on is surprising me. I'm gradually being brought down until two different wolves come and help me. Its Sawyer and Lane, the two of them had a light earthy colored coat that sparkled in the daylight. They each took off each maverick in turn and assisted me with support up. We remain in a triangle confronting the mavericks before us. They growl and snarl at us yet don't assault presently, its like they are hanging tight for a sign. All of the unexpected there was an extremely noisy cry that came from one of the fighters. It was anything but a whimper for an injurgy, it was a cry of death. At that point the gathering of rebels charge towards us. The three of us take them on and are winning until the rebels that Sawyer and Lane are battling quit battling them and begin coming towards me. These rebels were gigantic snd were unadulterated muscle. You would hope to have the option to beat them as a completely prepared wolf, however maybe they were super fighters. Sawyer and Lane follow them and battle them together this time and gradually advance. However, these rebels were so solid. While I battle two mavericks all at once I don't see one more coming at me prepared to take my life and that is when Sawyer bounces infront of me shielding me from the risk. I freeze, Sawyer has forfeited her life for me. My mom that I had as of late met has left me again however this time it was super durable. Path feels his association with his mate dissapear and he yells as clearly as conceivable communicating his greif. Every one of the heroes turn upward from what they are doing and notice Sawyers body on the ground and cry with him. Jax and I before long go along with them in their tune.

Path is hopeless, as an alpha your feelings are somewhat increased than others however as Alpha King it is twice as uplifted. Path doesn't race to assault the maverick that killed his mate. He strolls towards him, gradually, and sets down in front giving him simple admittance to his throat.

I bark at him and afterward mindlink him, Luka! Path! Try not to do this please!

Please accept my apologies Alice, yet I can't carry on with a daily existence where my mate doesn't exist in it. I told her the day of our mating service that any place she went I would follow. What's more I am a man of my assertion. I love you. He got done with saying before the maverick s;ashes his throat making Lanes body limp. Presently it was my chance to yell, then, at that point, immedeately, all I see is red.


    The End.